# THIS BIG WILD WORLD
## of pretty little things

written by
Danny and Mandy Glaser
Illustrated by
Mandy Glaser

This is a work of fiction. Names, characters, locations, and incidents are all works of the author's imagination. Any resemblance to any persons, living or dead, is strictly a coincidence.

THE BIG WILD WORLD OF PRETTY LITTLE THINGS Copyright © 2021 Line by Lion Publications
Illustrations Copyright © Mandy Sue Glaser
ISBN 978-1-948807-36-4

All rights reserved. No part of this publication may be reproduced, distributed, or transmitted in any form or by any means, including photocopying, recording, or other electronic or mechanical methods without the prior written permission of the publisher, except in the case of brief quotations embodied in critical reviews and certain other noncommercial uses permitted by copyright law. Thank you for respecting artists' rights.

LINE BY LION
PUBLICATIONS

Dedicated to Dale Springer (1952 – 2020)

Such a pretty little thing with its moonlit wings

A luna moth
in the dark
resting upon walnut bark

"Bark!" said the fox with joyful glee
when he met the moth 'neath the walnut tree

And he floated to the moon...

As the moon circles us
we circle the sun

And the fox on the farm keeps the mice on the run

But the mouse hides between the leaves

In the patch of shy violets
safe between the trees

The trees are singing, flowers swirl and bend

Colors dancing with a springtime friend

Friends with petals, friends with feathers
the wind blows all that is not tethered

Blowing clouds across the sky
flocks of swallows at sundown fly

Below the sky, deep in the ocean
the wind doesn't blow but the sea's in motion

Plumes of plankton drift and sway
and tides ebb and flow throughout the day

"Watch out! Watch out!" shouts the spotted trout
"He'll gulp all the fish down without a doubt!"

"Dive to the bottom for goodness sake!
There's a long-legged bird on the shore of the lake!"

On the bank of the lake in the forest of birches

A bear's hunting berries
an owl silently perches

"WHO?" hoots the horned owl
golden eyes glisten

"Not me," hopes the hiding hare
tall ears listen

Rabbits in the canyon can rarely find plants to hide their tails behind

But between the bluffs they burrow fine
in the layers shown by rain and time

The time for desert rain can be short and quite quick and the mud that was made may soon dry up like brick

So the tortoise and plants store raindrops inside
to last through the days of summer sunlight

Warm sunlight streams down on the green snake's skin
with his head in the clouds he begins to sing

"I'd fly all around if I only had wings!
I'd fly all around and see every little thing!
If I only had wings, I'd fly all the way around
this big wild world of pretty little things!"

### Host Plant
A plant that an animal or insect lives on or eats. The walnut tree is a host plant for luna moths along with other trees, such as hickory, sweet gum, birch, persimmon and sumac. The caterpillar eats the leaves of these trees.

### Metamorphosis
The process of transforming from an immature to a mature stage, such as a tadpole to a frog and caterpillar into a butterfly. Amphibians and insects undergo metamorphosis.

### Pupa
The life stage some insects go through when they are inactive, between the time they are an immature insect and their mature form. An example of the pupal stage would be the time when the monarch caterpillar is changing into its adult form of the butterfly in a chrysalis. Only insects that undergo complete metamorphosis have a pupal stage. They are called **holometabolous** insects, because of their four life stages; egg, lavae, pupa, and adult (**imago**).

### Cocoon
Is the outside case or shell that protects the insect while in the pupal stage. Cocoons can be soft or hard. Many insects create cocoons, such as beetles, wasps, bees, flies and ants.

### Chrysalis
Is the cocoon that butterflies make.

### Nocturnal
Animals and insects that are active at night, such as the luna moth and fox.

### Diurnal
Animals and insects that are active during the day. Examples are birds, squirrels and pollinators, such as bees and butterflies.

### Crepuscular
Animals and insects that are active mainly during twilight periods. Crepuscular animals can also be active when daylight hours are overcast and when the night is well lit by the moon. Examples are animals such as house cats, deers and rabbits. Foxes can be crepuscular, but they are mostly nocturnal.

### Scotopic Vision
Being able to see in low light or at night, which is what nocturnal animals have.

### Photopic Vision
Being able to see in bright light conditions or daylight, which is the vision that diurnal animals have.

### Omnivore
An omnivore is an animal that eats both plants and meat. A bear is an omnivore because it eats a variety of plant and animal foods; including berries and fish. Are you an omnivore? Many humans are...

### Herbivore
A herbivore is an animal who only eats plant foods; such as fruits, seeds, grass and leaves. Some examples of herbivores are rabbits and tortoises.

### Carnivore
A carnivore is an animal that relies solely on meat for food. Snakes are carnivores because they eat small mammals, fish, and even insects!

### Predator
A predator is a hunter. An owl is a nocturnal predator.

### Prey
Prey is what a predator is hunting for. A mouse is the prey of many predators, including foxes, owls and snakes.

### Pollen
The powdery dust-like substance that is inside plants, sometimes it is yellow. It is actually micropores, and is the substance that makes it possible for plants to reproduce. Wind, animals and insects, such as bees carry the pollen from a male flower to a female flower.

### Pollinator
An animal or anything that moves pollen from one part of a plant to another.

### Seed Dispersal
The movement or spreading of seeds away from the parent plant. Wind and animals both play a part. Wind can carry seeds, bird droppings can disperse seeds, and burr-like seeds can be carried on animal fur because their burr seed pod functions as a hook.

### Succulent
A plant that stores water in its leaves or stems. Usually the leaves are thick and fleshy. Cacti and aloe are examples of succulents. Succulents thrive in dry environments, such as deserts.

### Molting

The process of shedding or casting off skin, feathers, hair and horns. This aids invertebrates, such as insects to shed their outer layer so they can grow. It allows reptiles and amphibians to grow new skin, and birds to grow new feathers. Mammals also molt by shedding their winter coats, and some mammals even grow new horns and antlers, such as deer.

### Invertebrates
An animal without a backbone, such as insects, **crustaceans** (an example is a shrimp) or **mollusks** (an example is a snail).

# About the Artist and Author

Mandy and Danny met in Savannah, GA while attending Savannah College of Art and Design.

They've spent time living in Austin, Texas, but now reside in Kentucky where they have two children, Rosie and Harlan. Danny is a firefighter and Mandy is a stay-at-home mom. Together they are pursuing their dreams of having a small farm, raising kids, and camping.

Mandy is currently working on illustrating another children's book that combines nature and science, as well as a photography project called, "Rosie the Mammal and Harlan the Animal: Tales From A Mother Without A Tribe".

## Also by Line by Lion

Mice in the Mill
The Fairies' Ball
Hannah However
Meanwhile Miles
It's a Cold, Cold Day
Mallory and the Dragon
A Little Fish Told Me

Ne Ne'e and BoBo Love you very much. XOXO ♡

CPSIA information can be obtained
at www.ICGtesting.com
Printed in the USA
LVHW071701110721
692411LV00004BA/24